FLOWER·FAIRIES
OF THE SUMMER

FLOWER·FAIRIES
OF THE SUMMER

SUMMER

Poems and pictures by

CICELY MARY BARKER

FREDERICK WARNE

FREDERICK WARNE

Published by the Penguin Group
Penguin Books Ltd, 80 Strand, London WC2R 0RL, England
Penguin Putnam Inc., 375 Hudson Street, New York, N.Y. 10014, USA
Penguin Books Australia Ltd, 250 Camberwell Road, Camberwell,
Victoria 3124, Australia
Penguin Books Canada Ltd, 10 Alcorn Avenue, Toronto, Ontario, Canada M4V 3B2
Penguin Books (NZ) Ltd, Cnr Rosedale and Airborne Roads, Albany,
Auckland, New Zealand
Penguin Books India (P) Ltd, 11 Community Centre, Panchsheel Park,
New Delhi 110 017, India
Penguin Books (South Africa) (Pty) Ltd, PO Box 9, Parklands 2121, South Africa

Penguin Books Ltd, Registered Offices: 80 Strand, London WC2R 0RL, England

Web site at: www.flowerfairies.com

First published 1925
First published by Frederick Warne 1990
This edition first published 2002
1 3 5 7 9 10 8 6 4 2

ISBN 0 7232 4827 3

Printed in Hong Kong

CONTENTS

PLANTAIN AND MOON-DAISY DANCING TOGETHER,
ALL THROUGH THE BEAUTIFUL SUNSHINY WEATHER.

SPRING GOES, SUMMER COMES

The little darling, Spring,
    Has run away;
The sunshine grew too hot for her to stay.

She kissed her sister, Summer,
    And she said:
"When I am gone, you must be queen
  instead."

Now reigns the Lady Summer,
    Round whose feet
A thousand fairies flock with blossoms sweet.

The Buttercup Fairy

THE SONG OF
THE BUTTERCUP FAIRY

'Tis I whom children love the best;
    My wealth is all for them;
For them is set each glossy cup
    Upon each sturdy stem.

O little playmates whom I love!
    The sky is summer-blue,
And meadows full of buttercups
    Are spread abroad for you.

THE SONG OF
THE HERB ROBERT FAIRY

Little Herb Robert,
    Bright and small,
Peeps from the bank
    Or the old stone wall.

Little Herb Robert,
    His leaf turns red;
He's wild geranium,
    So it is said.

The Herb Robert Fairy

The Forget-me-not Fairy

THE SONG OF
THE FORGET-ME-NOT FAIRY

So small, so blue, in grassy places
　　My flowers raise
　　Their tiny faces.

By streams my bigger sisters grow,
　　And smile in gardens,
　　In a row.

I've never seen a garden plot;
　　But though I'm small
　　Forget me not!

THE SONG OF
THE POPPY FAIRY

The green wheat's a-growing,
 The lark sings on high;
In scarlet silk a-glowing,
 Here stand I.

The wheat's turning yellow,
 Ripening for sheaves;
I hear the little fellow
 Who scares the bird-thieves.

Now the harvest's ended,
 The wheat-field is bare;
But still, red and splendid,
 I am there.

The Poppy Fairy

The Foxglove Fairy

THE SONG OF
THE FOXGLOVE FAIRY

"Foxglove, Foxglove,
    What do you see?"
The cool green woodland,
    The fat velvet bee;
Hey, Mr Bumble,
    I've honey here for thee!

"Foxglove, Foxglove,
    What see you now?"
The soft summer moonlight
    On bracken, grass, and bough;
And all the fairies dancing
    As only they know how.

THE SONG OF
THE WILD ROSE FAIRY

I am the queen whom everybody knows:
    I am the English Rose;
As light and free as any Jenny Wren,
    As dear to Englishmen;
As joyous as a Robin Redbreast's tune,
    I scent the air of June;
My buds are rosy as a baby's cheek;
    I have one word to speak,
One word which is my secret and my song,
'Tis "England, England, England" all day long.

The Wild Rose Fairy

The White Clover Fairy

THE SONG OF
THE WHITE CLOVER FAIRY

I'm little White Clover, kind and clean;
Look at my threefold leaves so green;
Hark to the buzzing of hungry bees:
"Give us your honey, Clover, please!"

Yes, little bees, and welcome, too!
My honey is good, and meant for you!

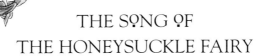

THE SONG OF
THE HONEYSUCKLE FAIRY

The lane is deep, the bank is steep,
  The tangled hedge is high;
And clinging, twisting, up I creep,
  And climb towards the sky.
O Honeysuckle, mounting high!
O Woodbine, climbing to the sky!

The people in the lane below
  Look up and see me there,
Where I my honey-trumpets blow,
  Whose sweetness fills the air.
O Honeysuckle, waving there!
O Woodbine, scenting all the air!

The Honeysuckle Fairy

The Bird's-Foot Trefoil Fairy

THE SONG OF
THE BIRD'S-FOOT TREFOIL FAIRY

Here I dance in a dress like flames,
And laugh to think of my comical names.
Hoppetty hop, with nimble legs!
Some folks call me *Bacon and Eggs*!
While other people, it's really true,
Tell me I'm *Cuckoo's Stockings* too!
Over the hill I skip and prance;
I'm *Lady's Slipper*, and so I dance,
Not like a lady, grand and proud,
But to the grasshoppers' chirping loud.
My pods are shaped like a dicky's toes:
That is what *Bird's-Foot Trefoil* shows;
This is my name which grown-ups use,
But children may call me what they choose.

THE SONG OF
THE NIGHTSHADE FAIRY

My name is Nightshade, also Bittersweet;
    Ah, little folk, be wise!
Hide you your hands behind you when we meet,
    Turn you away your eyes.
My flowers you shall not pick, nor berries eat,
    For in them poison lies.

(Though this is so poisonous, it is not the Deadly Nightshade,
but the Woody Nightshade. The berries turn red a little later on.)

The Nightshade Fairy

The Harebell Fairy

THE SONG OF
THE HAREBELL FAIRY

O bells, on stems so thin and fine!
   No human ear
   Your sound can hear,
O lightly chiming bells of mine!

When dim and dewy twilight falls,
   Then comes the time
   When harebells chime
For fairy feasts and fairy balls.

They tinkle while the fairies play,
   With dance and song,
   The whole night long,
Till daybreak wakens, cold and grey,
And elfin music fades away.

(The Harebell is the Bluebell of Scotland.)

THE SONG OF
THE HEATHER FAIRY

"Ho, Heather, ho! From south to north
Spread now your royal purple forth!
Ho, jolly one! From east to west,
The moorland waiteth to be dressed!"

I come, I come! With footsteps sure
I run to clothe the waiting moor;
From heath to heath I leap and stride
To fling my bounty far and wide.

(The heather in the picture is bell heather, or heath; it is
different from the common heather which is also called ling.)

The Heather Fairy

The Yarrow Fairy

THE SONG OF
THE YARROW FAIRY

Among the harebells and the grass,
  The grass all feathery with seed,
I dream, and see the people pass:
  They pay me little heed.

And yet the children (so I think)
  In spite of other flowers more dear,
Would miss my clusters white and pink,
  If I should disappear.

(The Yarrow has another name, Milfoil, which means
Thousand Leaf; because her leaves are all made up of very
many tiny little leaves.)

THE SONG OF
THE TOADFLAX FAIRY

The children, the children,
    they call me funny names,
They take me for their darling
    and partner in their games;
They pinch my flowers' yellow mouths,
    to open them and close,
Saying, *Snap-Dragon!*
       Toadflax!
          or, *darling Bunny-Nose!*

The Toadflax, the Toadflax,
    with lemon-coloured spikes,
With funny friendly faces
    that everybody likes,
Upon the grassy hillside
    and hedgerow bank it grows,
And it's *Snap-Dragon!*
       Toadflax!
          and *darling Bunny-Nose!*

The Toadflax Fairy

The Scabious Fairy

THE SONG OF
THE SCABIOUS FAIRY

Like frilly cushions full of pins
For tiny dames and fairykins;

Or else like dancers decked with gems,
My flowers sway on slender stems.

They curtsey in the meadow grass,
And nod to butterflies who pass.

THE SONG OF
THE SCARLET PIMPERNEL FAIRY

By the furrowed fields I lie,
Calling to the passers-by:
"If the weather you would tell,
Look at Scarlet Pimpernel."

When the day is warm and fine,
I unfold these flowers of mine;
Ah, but you must look for rain
When I shut them up again!

Weather-glasses on the walls
Hang in wealthy people's halls:
Though I lie where cart-wheels pass
I'm the Poor Man's Weather-Glass!

The Scarlet Pimpernel Fairy

The Greater Knapweed Fairy

THE SONG OF
THE GREATER KNAPWEED FAIRY

Oh, please, little children, take note of my
    name:
To call me a thistle is really a shame:
I'm harmless old Knapweed, who grows
    on the chalk,
I never will prick you when out for your
    walk.

Yet I should be sorry, yes, sorry indeed,
To cut your small fingers and cause them
    to bleed;
So bid me Good Morning when out for
    your walk,
And mind how you pull at my very tough
    stalk.

(Sometimes this Knapweed is called Hardhead; and he has a
brother, the little Knapweed, whose flower is not quite like this.)

THE SONG OF
THE TRAVELLER'S JOY FAIRY

Traveller, traveller, tramping by
To the seaport town where the big ships lie,
See, I have built a shady bower
To shelter you from the sun or shower.
Rest for a bit, then on, my boy!
Luck go with you, and Traveller's Joy!

Traveller, traveller, tramping home
From foreign places beyond the foam,
See, I have hung out a white festoon
To greet the lad with the dusty shoon.
Somewhere a lass looks out for a boy:
Luck be with you, and Traveller's Joy!

(Traveller's Joy is Wild Clematis; and when the flowers are over,
it becomes a mass of silky fluff, and then we call it Old-Man's-Beard.)

The Traveller's Joy Fairy

The Ragwort Fairy

THE SONG OF
THE RAGWORT FAIRY

Now is the prime of Summer past,
  Farewell she soon must say;
But yet my gold you may behold
  By every grassy way.

And what though Autumn comes apace,
  And brings a shorter day?
Still stand I here, your eyes to cheer,
  In gallant gold array.

THE SONG OF
THE ROSE FAIRY

Best and dearest flower that grows,
Perfect both to see and smell;
Words can never, never tell
Half the beauty of a Rose—
Buds that open to disclose
Fold on fold of purest white,
Lovely pink, or red that glows
Deep, sweet-scented. What delight
   To be Fairy of the Rose!

The Rose Fairy

Also by Cicely Mary Barker

Flower Fairies of the Spring
Flower Fairies of the Autumn
Flower Fairies of the Winter
Flower Fairies of the Trees
Flower Fairies of the Garden
Flower Fairies of the Wayside
A Flower Fairy Alphabet